*Persea gratissima*

2.    4.    6.    7.

# Other books by John Burningham

# Avocado
# Baby

*John Burningham*

RED FOX

*For Emms*

A Red Fox Book

Published by Random House Children's Books
61-63 Uxbridge Road, London W5 5SA

A division of The Random House Group Ltd
London Melbourne Sydney Auckland
Johannesburg and agencies throughout the world

Copyright © John Burningham 1982

9 10 8

First published in Great Britain in 1982 by Jonathan Cape Ltd
This Red Fox edition 2000

Printed in Singapore by Tien Wah Press (PTE) Ltd

THE RANDOM HOUSE GROUP Limited Reg. No. 954009
www.kidsatrandomhouse.co.uk

ISBN 978 0 099 20061 1

Mr and Mrs Hargraves and their two children
were not very strong. Mrs Hargraves was
expecting another baby, and they all hoped
it would not be as weak as they were.

The new baby was born and all the family were very pleased. Mr and Mrs Hargraves brought the baby home and it grew but, as they feared, it did not grow strong.

Mrs Hargraves found
feeding the baby very difficult.
It did not like food or want to eat much.

"Whatever can I do," wailed Mrs Hargraves. "The baby doesn't like eating anything I make and it looks so weak."

"Why don't you give it that avocado pear?" said the children.

In the fruit bowl on the table there was an avocado pear. Nobody knew how it had got there because the Hargraves never bought avocados. Mrs Hargraves cut the pear in half, mashed it and gave it to the baby, who ate it all up.

From that day on an amazing thing happened. The baby became very strong.

It was getting so strong it could

break out from the straps
on its high chair,

pull other children uphill in a cart,

wrench off the side of its cot.
And each day Mrs Hargraves gave
the baby avocado pear.

One night a burglar got into the house.

The baby woke up and, hearing the burglar
moving about downstairs, leapt out of its cot.

The baby picked up
a broom, and chased
the burglar.

The burglar was so frightened at being chased by a baby that he dropped his bag and ran out of the house.

The next day Mr Hargraves put a notice on the gate. "That should keep the burglars away," he said.

The baby would help
carry the shopping,

move the furniture

and push the car
when it would
not start.

One day two bullies were waiting
for the children in the park.

The bullies started
being very nasty to
the children.

The baby did not like that and jumped out
of its push-chair,

picked up the bullies and

threw them into the pond.

The baby gets stronger every day and of course it is still eating avocado pears.

*Persea gratissima*